PENNY IN THE ROAD

KATHARINE WILSON PRECEK

ILLUSTRATED BY
PATRICIA CULLEN-CLARK

MACMILLAN PUBLISHING COMPANY
NEW YORK

SOUTH HUNTINGTON
PUBLIC LIBRARY
2 MELVILLE ROAD
HUNTINGTON STATION, N.Y. 11746

Precek

Text copyright © 1989 by Katharine Precek
Illustrations copyright © 1989 by Patricia Cullen-Clark

All rights reserved. No part of this book may be reproduced or
transmitted in any form or by any means, electronic or mechanical,
including photocopying, recording, or by any information storage and
retrieval system, without permission in writing from the Publisher.

Macmillan Publishing Company
866 Third Avenue, New York, NY 10022
Collier Macmillan Canada, Inc.
Printed and bound in Japan
First American Edition

10 9 8 7 6 5 4 3 2 1

The text of this book is set in 16 point Bodoni Book.
The illustrations are rendered in blended Prismacolor and pastel on board.

Library of Congress Cataloging-in-Publication Data
Precek, Katharine.
Penny in the road/by Katharine Precek;
illustrated by Patricia Cullen-Clark.—1st American ed.
p.   cm.
Summary: A boy who finds an old penny on a country road
in 1913 imagines the daily life of the boy who might have
dropped it in 1793 and contrasts it with his own life.
ISBN 0-02-774970-3
[1. United States—Social life and customs—1783-1865—Fiction.
2. United States—Social life and customs—1865-1918—Fiction.]
I. Cullen-Clark, Patricia, ill. II. Title.
PZ7.P907Pe 1989   [E]—dc 19
88-13331 CIP AC

263709

To my husband, RICK,
and to our children,
IAN, JOSHUA, and MEGAN,
with love
—K.W.P.

For R.R.C. and J.L.C.
—P.C.C.

A long time ago when I was a young boy, I walked a country road to school. The road was old, even older than the Pennsylvania fieldstone houses on either side, for it had once been an Indian trail.

I carried my schoolbooks tied at the end of a strap I held over my shoulder, and I swung my tin lunch pail from my other hand as I walked. The black rubber galoshes my mother made me wear were splattered with mud from springtime puddles.

As I waded through one puddle that was especially wide, I watched the red mud swirl up like smoke around my feet. I noticed something flat and round and dark dislodge from the puddle bottom and then sink down again. I set my lunch pail on a dry spot in the road, crouched down, and felt through the cold, gooey mud with my fingers. I hoped what I had seen was a button or a bottle cap. Finally I felt and grasped it and swished my hand through the water to clean off the mud.

I opened my hand, and there, glistening wet, was a large brown coin. On one side was a wreath with the words *One Cent* in the middle and *United States of America* around the outside edge. On the other side was the head of a lady with long flowing hair. Above her was the word *Liberty* and beneath her the date *1793*.

I stood in the middle of the puddle looking at the penny, and my heart pounded with excitement at what I had found. I wondered how long the penny might have lain there in the road. Farm wagons and fancy carriages must have driven over it. Covered wagons heading west might have rattled right on top of it.

Who might have dropped the penny? Maybe a boy in a three-cornered hat lost it through a hole in the pocket of his breeches. The coin might have lain there in the road all that time until I found it in the mud.

I checked my pocket to make sure it had no hole, carefully put the penny down inside, and buttoned the flap over so the penny couldn't fall out. I walked on to school, and I thought about the boy who might have dropped the penny.

A boy in 1793 wouldn't be wearing rubber galoshes and carrying books to school on such a fine spring day. He would be barefooted, wearing linen knee breeches and a calico shirt. Up and down the broad fields that bordered the road he walked, flicking the reins and talking to the plow horse. As he plowed the moist earth of his father's farm, he watched for worms. Later maybe he would go fishing.

I sat at my desk at school and tried to study spelling, but I kept thinking of the boy who lost the penny.

When his father didn't need him on the farm, he had to go to school. He sat on a hard, long bench with the other boys his age and studied spelling words from a slate. He had to stand and recite his lesson to a stern-faced schoolmaster who wore wire-rimmed glasses and a ruffled shirt.

At noon recess I sat on the steps with my friends and ate my sandwich. I finished my oatmeal cookies and then played baseball with the other boys. I wondered what a boy in knee breeches and a three-cornered hat did at noon recess.

A dipper of water from the well and two corn cakes split and spread with molasses made a fine lunch for a boy in 1793. After he ate, he ran foot races with his friends, or played hide-and-seek. Or maybe he played with marbles made of clay glazed in rich brown, red, and yellow colors.

After school I said good-bye to my friends at the bottom of the hill and started up the long dirt road. I had not told anyone about finding the penny. I took it out of my pocket and looked at it while I walked.

I was thinking about the boy who might have dropped it, when all of a sudden I heard a tremendous noise coming up the road behind me. I turned around fast, and there, headed right for me, was a shiny black delivery truck. It stopped right next to me, and inside was Mr. Bailey, the grocer from town. A sign on the side of the truck said *Bailey's Grocery* in fancy gold letters.

While I told Mr. Bailey where I'd found the penny, I could see he was thinking of something. He reached around the dark green leather seat and took a small box from a crate.

"Would you like to trade it?" he asked, and he opened the box. There, nestled in shiny white satin, was a beautiful pearl-handled jackknife. Mr. Bailey handed it to me. "Here. Open it up and see what you think," he said.

It was the very jackknife I had seen last month in Bailey's Grocery. All of us boys at school wanted one. It had six blades and was the fanciest knife I'd ever seen. I looked at the penny and held the smooth, cool knife. I thought about it hard for a few minutes, and then slowly I handed the knife back to Mr. Bailey.

"I guess I'd rather have the penny, sir," I told him. I was afraid he'd be mad, but Mr. Bailey smiled.

"I'm glad you realize that this coin is more important than a jackknife. You're a smart boy." He handed me the penny and started up the truck's engine. Even though I was sorry about not having the jackknife, I felt good about keeping the penny. Up the hill we went in that bumpy, noisy, wonderful truck.

At the road to our farm Mr. Bailey stopped. "So long, now. Say hello to your folks. And take good care of that penny." I thanked him and watched as he drove the delivery truck away.

Walking under the big trees that lined the road, I thought about my penny. A boy in 1793 might have walked this same road, but no delivery truck would have given him a ride.

A tin peddler might have pulled his horse to a stop, though, and given the boy a ride. The boy climbed up behind the big red and yellow wheel and sat on the wooden wagon seat beside the peddler. As they jingled along, he showed the peddler his penny, and the peddler showed the boy all the things he could buy.

A shiny set of bread pans for his mother, a bright new pail for his father, and a set of toy soldiers were among the wares the peddler displayed. The boy stared at those little soldiers in their blue and buff and red coats and wished he could buy them. But the boy shook his head no; he was saving his penny for something else.

He got down from the peddler's cart and waved good-bye. As he walked on up the road, he put his penny in his pocket. And maybe that is when the penny fell through a hole and the boy lost it.

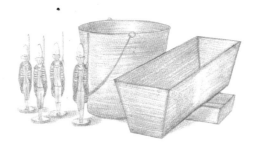

I never did trade that penny. I kept it safe in a little red sack in my top dresser drawer for many years. I grew up and got married and had a family. When my children were young, I gathered them around me and showed them the penny. I told them about a boy in 1793 who lost it, and about a boy in 1913 who found it.

My children grew up, and when they had children I became a grandfather. Now sometimes when I visit them I bring along the little red sack. I let my grandchildren hold the penny, and I tell them about the boy in a three-cornered hat who lost it, and about the boy in rubber galoshes who found it one spring day in a puddle on an old country road.

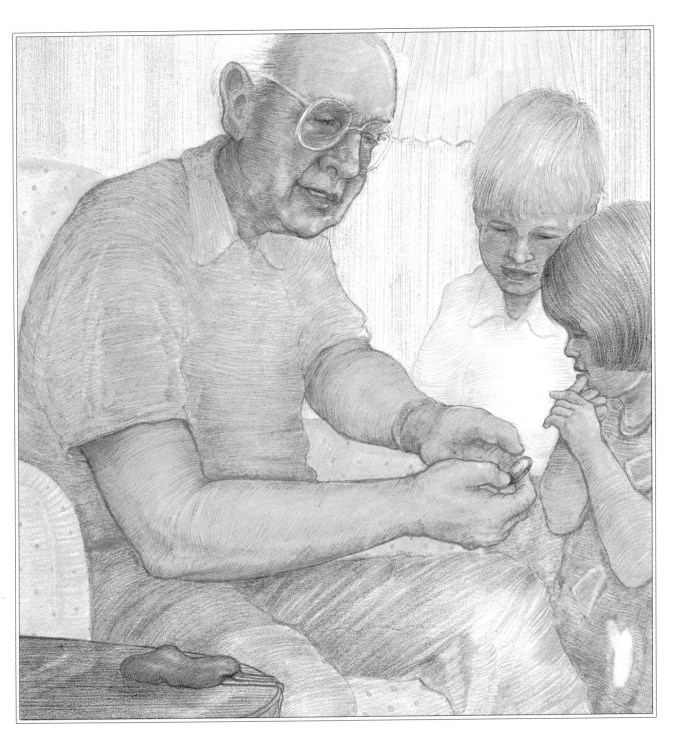

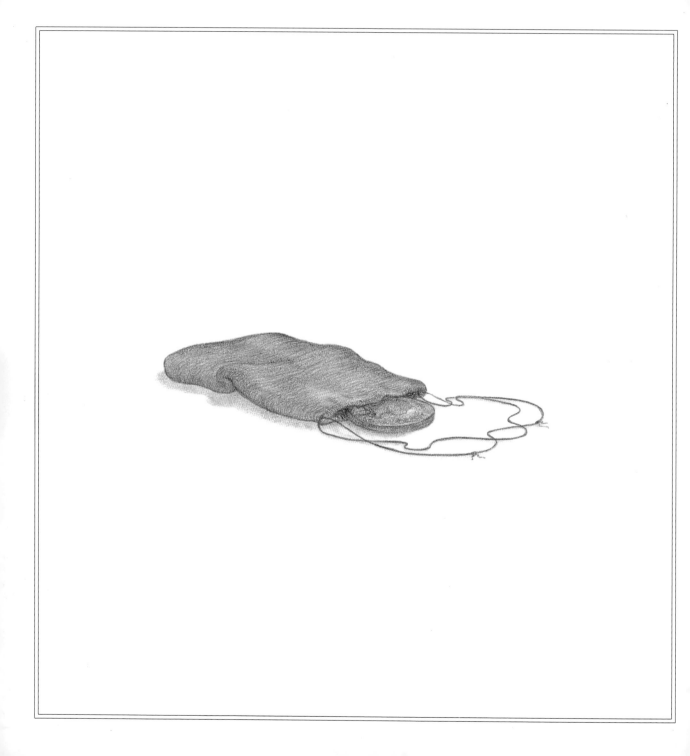

PRECEK   11/22/89
PENNY IN THE ROAD
(0) 1989 J PRE
0652   03 799771   01 9   (IC=1)

B065203799771019B

2C3702

J   Precek, Katharine
PRE   Wilson

         Penny in the road

$14.95

DATE		

MAY 1 8 1989

SOUTH HUNTINGTON
PUBLIC LIBRARY
2 MELVILLE ROAD
HUNTINGTON STATION, N.Y. 11746

© THE BAKER & TAYLOR CO.